MR MAGUS IS WAITING FOR YOU

by the same author

Stories about Cricklepit Combined School

THE TURBULENT TERM OF TYKE TILER
(Awarded the Library Association's Carnegie Medal)
GOWIE CORBY PLAYS CHICKEN
CHARLIE LEWIS PLAYS FOR TIME
(Runner-up for the Whitbread Award)
JUNIPER: A Mystery

JASON BODGER AND THE PRIORY GHOST
NO PLACE LIKE
DOG DAYS AND CAT NAPS
THE CLOCK TOWER GHOST
THE WELL
THE PRIME OF TAMWORTH PIG
TAMWORTH PIG SAVES THE TREES
TAMWORTH PIG AND THE LITTER
CHRISTMAS WITH TAMWORTH PIG

Edited by Gene Kemp

DUCKS AND DRAGONS
Poems for Children

GENE KEMP

MR. MAGUS IS WAITING FOR YOU.

illustrations by Alan Baker

faber and faber
LONDON · BOSTON

THAMES TELEVISION
LONDON

First published in 1986
by Faber and Faber Limited
3 Queen Square London WC1N 3AU
and Thames Television Limited
149 Tottenham Court Road London W1P 9LL

Photoset by Parker Typesetting Service, Leicester
Printed in Great Britain by
Richard Clay Ltd Bungay Suffolk

British Library Cataloguing in Publication Data

Kemp, Gene
Mr Magus is waiting for you.
I. Title
823'.914[J] PZ7
ISBN 0-571-14686-4
ISBN 0-571-14687-2 Pbk

Chapter One

'HERE I come! Fantastic! GOAL!' shouted Jeff Stanner at the top of his voice. 'CRACK!' The noise of the window answering back was even louder as it fractured into a thousand glittering splinters, followed by an outraged howl from inside but Jeff wasn't waiting any more, for he was running with great speed and concentration, leaping over the back wall into the alley way and then into the street beyond. Behind him, sobbing fatly, ran – if you could call it running – his pal, Vince. Running wasn't Vince's thing. Neither was football for that matter, but he got nagged, bullied, persuaded into it by Jeff, a fitness freak with a little talent, though not as much as he thought he had. Vince's idea of hell was PE lessons and as his teacher pointed out he used more time and energy thinking up excuses for getting out of Games than he would have done if he'd actually played.

What Vince actually liked were insects, anything that crawled, hopped, flew, bit etc. He was mad about insects, the only things he really knew anything about. He couldn't understand why Jeff always dragged him along with him. Neither did Jeff. They had nothing in common, but they'd known each other since they'd screamed at each other in their buggies and now were in the same class at school, Millington Community School. Enough. Vince had to tag along and save Jeff's shots. But he often missed. Witness the broken window.

Jeff paused, listening for sounds of pursuit. His Dad had a terrible temper and this wasn't the first time that window had gone bust. But the afternoon on Mayflower Housing Estate was quiet, except for cries and noises from the nearby park. He leaned back against a wall and waited for Vince to catch up with him.

It was a hot grey day, heavy with a hint of thunder, the tail end of the summer holidays, following a wet August in which nothing much seemed to have happened, except for news of pop stars quarrelling, and bombs and disasters. Almost, Jeff and Vince would be glad to get back to school although they wouldn't have admitted this.

'Why didn't you save that one? It wasn't one of my super shots, was it?' he asked when Vince finally caught up with him.

'It was too high,' muttered Vince between panting and sweating. He wore a thick pullover and anorak which he refused to take off, ever, except when his Mum forcibly removed them.

'Well, we've done it now. The last thing my Dad told me was not to touch that window. The putty's not dry yet, he said. From last week when we broke it. It's a good job he didn't catch us. He'd have half killed us.'

Vince wasn't listening. Some flying ants were setting off from the wall they were leaning against and he was far more interested in them. Jeff's Dad's terrible temper was Jeff's problem. He'd got enough of his own with his mother, who still hoped and tried to shape Vince into something like the kind of boy she'd wanted, neat, hardworking and reliable. Vince kept telling her it was a waste of time but she hadn't given up yet.

'We'll go to the park,' announced Jeff. He always decided where they would go and Vince tagged along, not much bothered. Insects can be found in most places.

'I don't want to go without my ball, though. Must get some practice in before next term. But I daren't go back in the house again yet.

'I know,' he went on. 'My brother's got a ball in the shed. He never uses it these days. I'll get that. It'll be OK as long as he doesn't find out. He hates me having anything of his, mean pig. You hang on here, Vince. Shan't be a tick.'

He disappeared at speed. Vince hardly noticed him go. He'd found an ant colony living and thriving, bustling about in a crack in the pavement. Vince liked their tiny community. Soon he was bending down with the magnifying glass he always carried in his back pocket and examining them. A passing dog sniffed at him, but Vince just kicked out an irritable foot at it and went on studying the ants, so busy, so industrious.

Chapter Two

Millington Park is very long and thin, a stretched out park. This is because it's a long disused railway line, grassed over, planted with trees and shrubs, and provided with seats, roundabouts and swings. Where once the old steam trains thundered past, children now play and you can imagine yourself in real country though traffic rumbles in the distance and planes fly overhead.

At the same time that Jeff Stanner was breaking a window and making his father furious, Tracey Lemayne and Charlie Tibbs lay on the grass in the peace and quiet of a timeless afternoon in the last week of the summer holidays.

Charlie was happy. An untidy heap in an old skirt and boy's shirt with scruffy hair, scrubby knees and inky fingers, granny specs half-way down her nose, she was reading an old and tatty paperback which she'd already read a dozen times 'cause it was great. She carried it everywhere with her in case she was stuck with somebody or something boring and then she could take out her book, draw its curtains round her, step into adventure country and forget the everyday, ordinary world.

But Tracey was not happy. She was a pretty girl with highlighted blonde hair, wearing sleepers in her ears for she'd just had them pierced. Unlike Charlie she was well turned out in tee shirt and calf-length jeans, lots of thin bracelets and carrying a Big Bag. But Tracey was bored.

Sometimes she didn't know why she still came out any more with old Charlie, who was only interested in books and kids stuff. It was just that they always went around together. They were in the same class at school. Their mothers were friends. They lived near each other. And they were quite different people. But nearly always together.

Tracey had taken lately to thinking about boys. Soon she hoped she'd be old enough for boys to notice her like they noticed her sister, who was sixteen and gorgeous. In the meantime Tracey day-dreamed, imagining herself strolling along by the side of a river, swans swimming on it, birds singing, a waterfall, a castle in the distance and a boy, dishy, handsome, strong, looking just like her favourite pop star and telling her how much he loved her, she was the most beautiful girl he'd ever seen in all his life. Instead of which here she was stuck with old Charlie in Millington Park, about as exciting as a wet Sunday afternoon in February. What was the point of doing herself up as she'd just done, new jeans, her sister's sweater – she'd be hopping mad when she found out, only Tracey intended getting it back before then – to sit here on the grass and watch Charlie reading that stupid paperback that she'd already read half a dozen times?

Charlie had just arrived at an exciting place where the heroine, a boyish girl, small and thin, called Sandy, rescues the expedition trapped in the collapsing cave with the tide coming in. Only her presence of mind and courage could save the day . . . and now the heroine, Sandy – you wouldn't know whether she was a boy or girl, Charlie liked that . . . was just gonna do her bit . . . when Tracey's voice broke in. Charlie was fond of old Trace but she'd got the imagination of a vegetable. Her ideas hardly went beyond whether she should wear her yellow tee-shirt or the blue one, or should she wear ten bangles or thirty-one?

'What d'you say, Trace?'

'I *knew* you weren't listening. Aren't you interested in boys at all?'

'No, not much. I want to get back to school. I'm more interested in that. Dead boring, these summer holidays. Dunno why. Perhaps it was the weather. Raining all the time.'

'I didn't get any tan this year. Not like last year. And we didn't go away. No money, my Mum said. Oh, I wish something would happen.'

It wasn't so much boys that Tracey wanted, it was adventure or something different happening. Reading about adventures, as Charlie did, wasn't the same for Tracey. She wanted the real thing.

Charlie went back to her book. Now that was really interesting. You didn't feel bored reading about adventures. Pity Tracey didn't read. It'd take her mind off boys. And her face. She was always investigating her own face. Even now, Charlie saw, looking up, that she'd got a mirror out of that Big Bag she carried and was patting her hair, adjusting her sleepers, smoothing her lips. Charlie returned to the swirling waters in the darkening cave. Sandy was about to do her bit. Charlie was hooked.

Tracey exploded . . .

'Oh, for Pete's sake. You gonna sit there all afternoon reading that stupid book? Let's go somewhere, *do* something, anything!'

There was no help for it. She'd have to go and hang round with Trace to see if there was anything at all going on in the park.

'Oh, all right. Let's split.'

She stuffed her book and her granny specs in her

pockets and they set off, following the high fence that ran all along that side of the park.

Chapter Three

'I'm knackered,' groaned Vince, crashing out on the grass near the high fence that ran round that side of Millington Park. Jeff, not winded at all, did some press-ups and then started to play around with the ball, which he did well. Vince watched in disgust, groaned again and then rolled over to investigate the insect life, busy in the grass just a few inches from his nose. As Jeff continued to play around with the ball, Vince fished out his magnifying glass and turned it upon an insect that had caught his attention.

'You're so shattered because you're a fatso,' Jeff said, flexing his muscles. 'Why don't you keep in shape like me?'

'Who wants to be a macho muscle man like you?' retorted Vince. 'It's so boring. Besides, I haven't got the time.'

'You. You don't do anything all day long.'

'Yes, I do. I'm learning how to be a scientist.'

'You're no good at Science at school.'

'That's different. I don't get much chance to study what I want there.'

'What? Creepy crawlies? Yuck.'

'Better than stupid football,' Vince muttered. Softly. He was always careful not to go too far with Jeff. He might get hurt.

'You gonna crash out there all afternoon?' asked Jeff at last, tiring of playing solo.

'What's wrong with that? It's the holidays, init?'

'Yeah, but it's school next week and I wanna get in

the team. So I need practice.'

'So, what's that got to do with me? I shan't get in any team if I practise till I drop dead.'

'Aw, comon, Vince. Be a pal.'

'Yuck,' answered Vince, but he got up all the same and stood against the wall.

'We need something for goal posts,' Jeff said. 'Give me your anorak.'

'No!'

Reluctantly he took it off and dropped it on the ground. Jeff threw down his sweater for the other post, took aim and slammed in a shot. It hit Vince hard, right in the chest.

'Ouch, that hurt!' cried Vince, turning to the wall and wrapping himself in waves of self-pity.

'Come on. It didn't hurt. Don't be such a wally.'

'Belt up,' muttered Vince.

Jeff dribbled the ball a bit then danced around.

'I'm the greatest –' he was just beginning when Tracey and Charlie came into sight.

Jeff wolf-whistled.

'Hey, Vince, get a load of that. I think she's great.'

Vince was not impressed. Like Jeff he'd known the girls from the days when they were all weighed in at the local clinic and to him they didn't look much different now. He knew Charlie slightly better than Tracey because they were in the same Maths group at school.

'Who, old Charlie?' he asked.

'No, you fool. Hi, Tracey.'

Glad that he was no longer required to play football, Vince thankfully flopped down and got out his magnifying glass once more, returning to his insects.

Now Jeff liked Tracey a lot but she seemed to look at him as if she found him beneath contempt (these days). She didn't bother to answer.

'Hi, Vince. Hi, Jeff,' said Charlie amiably. She didn't mind these two, they were old friends even if a bit stupid and boring.

Tracey was playing things very coolly. Privately she didn't think Jeff was bad-looking and at least he wasn't repulsive like Vince. But somehow, she didn't want him thinking she quite liked him, oh, no.

'Hi, Vince,' she said, ignoring Jeff.

This riled Jeff.

'What about me?'

'What about you?'

'I'm Jeff. Remember?'

Tracey shrugged and turned away as if anything that Jeff could do was of no interest to her whatsoever.

Chapter Four

In a room so high up that the tops of the trees waved below the windows, an old man waited, lying back in an old leather armchair, his beard flowing down on to his knees.

The room was deep and dark and comfortable, filled with books and maps, a globe and an astrolabe and other strange things. On the wall hung pictures filled, it seemed at first glance, with scenes from other countries and other centuries. If you looked closer it could be seen that the same man occurred in them over and over again. The man in the armchair.

On his lap, almost lost among the long silky beard, slept a black cat. Slowly the old man stroked the cat. A clock ticked quietly as they waited. Everything was still.

Chapter Five

'Here, get this,' said Vince, fishing out a matchbox and showing the insect inside it to Charlie who had flopped down beside him on the grass.

'Oh, it's weird. Wherja get it?'

'Found it just now. It's a new one on me. I'll have to look it up when I get back in.'

'Does it bite?'

'It hasn't bitten me yet. But I dunno. It might. Let's find out, eh?'

He jabbed a thumb at Tracey, who was busy showing Jeff that she wasn't in the least interested in him. Vince mimed putting the insect down her back and grinned wickedly. Charlie first shook her head then changed it to a nod. Serve Tracey right for showing off as if she was Miss World or Princess Diana. Tossing her head up and down like some batty pony.

'Go on. Wind her up.'

Jeff was doing his Special Football Show Off Exercise, where he dribbled the ball then ran it up and down each leg in turn. It was tricky and Jeff didn't do it badly. Actually he was wasting his time for soccer skills meant nothing at all to Tracey. He'd have done better playing a guitar except he wasn't musical.

'What you doing here?' he asked at last.

'Passing the time,' answered Tracey.

Taking a mirror out of the Big Bag she inspected the state of her sleepers.

Jeff was working up his courage.

'Doing anything special?'

'Maybe. Maybe not. What's it to you?'

Here goes, thought Jeff.

'I thought you might . . . come out with me some time.' There, he'd said it. He pulled out his sunglasses and put them on. It didn't matter that the sky was covered with grey and purple thunder clouds, the opaque lenses made him look older and more interesting, he thought.

'When did they let you out of play-school?' asked Tracey, turning away.

At that moment, Vince, creeping up, dropped the insect down Tracey's back. She screamed, wriggled, jumped up and down, pulling at her sister's sweater to get rid of it for creepy crawlies terrified her. Vince fell about laughing, but Jeff, generously, since she hadn't done a lot for him, said:

'Want me to thump him for you, Tracey?'

Perhaps it was Charlie grinning all over her face that decided Tracey not to lose her cool.

'Don't bother. He's just a wally.'

She hitched back the tee-shirt.

'Remember how we all used to play together?' asked Jeff.

'What? That old gang?' Tracey answered.

'What did we call ourselves? We had a name.'

'I don't remember,' said Tracey, although she did really.

Hearing this Charlie got up and joined them.

'I remember. The Nutters. Because we were crazy.'

Vince joined in.

'It got us into rows.'

His mother had once kept him in for a week after one of their exploits, which had brought the police round to his house. For when they were younger, every holiday the four of them were always together, holding meetings in Jeff's shed, plotting tricks and adventures, Jeff the leader, Vince trailing along last. But then it changed. This holiday it had been different. They didn't mix in the same way any more.

'We've grown out of that old rubbish now,' said Tracey. How boring, she thought.

'You can say that again,' Jeff replied, kicking the ball once more.

'Fantastic,' he yelled, giving it just that little extra.

He'd pitched it too high again.

It flew straight over the fence.

They all stared at the spot where it had flown over.

'Oh, heck,' moaned Jeff.

Tracey raised her eyes heavenwards.

'Oh, forget it,' she said, irritated with Jeff and his football.

'I can't. It's my big brother's.'

Vince began to take the mickey.

'Dearie me,' he quavered in a high-pitched voice. 'Is he six foot two, then?'

'No, six foot four and he'll kill me. I've got to get it back.'

He looked pleadingly at Tracey. If she came it wouldn't be too draggy.

'Come with me, you lot. Please, Trace.' He'd always called her Trace at one time.

Tracey and Charlie looked at one another.

'OK,' said Charlie. 'Why not?'

'Just for a giggle,' added Tracey, for after all there wasn't anything else to do, was there?

'Like the Nutters,' grinned Charlie.

'Let's find the best place to get over,' announced Jeff,

taking over the boss role as usual.

They wandered up along the fence looking for some spot where it could be climbed easily. But Vince hung back. He was hot and sweaty. He wanted to lie down and look at his insects. He didn't want to get into trouble trespassing. That had happened before with the Nutters gang. Not again. No thanks.

'Not me. No way,' he called after them.

'You're coming, Fatso, if I have to kick you over,' said Boss Jeff.

A minute later he spotted a corner where the fence was broken down.

'Here, over here, Tracey,' he called.

Chapter Six

In the room high above the tree-tops the old man stirred in his chair, disturbing the black cat, which yawned and stretched its limbs. The old man whispered into the cat's ear.

'It's beginning, Gib, my cat. It's beginning.'

The old man was called Mr Magus.

Chapter Seven

'Over here.'

'I can't.'

'It's easy.'

'For you, maybe.'

'Come on.'

'Don't make so much noise.'

'Ouch.'

In the end they all got over, Vince rolling a little, Tracey stately to the end, Jeff showing how easy it all was, Charlie scrambling, all of them making a fair amount of noise, not a good idea as Jeff said. But then they fell silent.

For they found themselves in a garden.

And what a garden. They hadn't seen anything like it before.

The garden was the world and the world was the garden. A world of waving trees and shrubs they hadn't known existed. Soft green lawns were surrounded by flowers of every colour and many scents. Petals drifted, blown by the breeze. Fruit hung from the trees, a lower branch of a huge old tree held a swing. A house could just be spotted through the roses, far away it seemed.

'The Garden of Eden,' thought Tracey.

Jeff's thoughts were on finding the ball.

'Didn't know all this was in season, at the same time,' thought Vince. 'Should be plenty of insects here.'

'Why does it remind me of a trap?' Charlie wondered. 'Perhaps it's too beautiful.'

They moved slowly in the direction of the house.

'I've got to find it,' muttered Jeff, searching among the bushes, a mammoth undertaking. 'Hey, someone, give me a hand.'

'You and your bloomin' ball,' said Vince, getting out his magnifying glass and beginning his own search.

'Look at that!' cried Tracey. 'I love swings.'

She slipped on to the seat and began to work it up high, flying to the clouds, far away from the others, lost in her own dreams. This was better. A million miles from Millington Park and a boring afternoon. Here, anything could happen, adventure, romance. Tracey was happy at last.

Charlie wandered off on her own, also lost in thought until she stopped still, quite suddenly and for no particular reason. She'd heard nothing, felt nothing but such a sensation of danger had swept over her that she was too scared to move, frozen like a rabbit by a snake. Something was wrong, something was bad, something was UP, definitely UP. She looked round. And found herself alone among trees which she couldn't recognize. No one was in sight. Nor could she hear the others. She might have been alone on an alien planet. A fit of shivering took her though the afternoon was close, heavy.

We shouldn't be here, she thought. It's not just trespassing. It's bad.

She hurried to join the others but couldn't immediately find them though she was sure they were near.

We've got to get out of here. We're in a trap, she thought wildly, and then, don't be stupid, you're imagining things, and what would Sandy, your heroine, do? She wouldn't stand there twitching in the bushes, would she? Charlie shook herself mentally and hurried on through the garden, coming unexpectedly

on a pool, covered with water lilies, plants cascading over the edge, and among them a statue of a stone cat with eyes that stared at her. She hated that cat.

Terrified, she ran for Tracey and found her just getting out of the swing.

'I had the funniest feeling up there,' said Tracey, joining her. 'I was swinging as high as that house, right up and away over the world. I like it.'

But Charlie's fear was still with her.

'I don't,' she said. 'We're trespassing and we could get done for it.'

Actually it wasn't so much the fear of trespassing that was worrying her as this other terror of being caught in something she couldn't understand. But she didn't want to say this, lest she made it real by talking about it and in case she was laughed at.

'No, we shan't get done,' said Tracey, all matter of fact. 'We're too young and there's no one here anyway. They're on holiday.'

'How do *you* know?'

Tracey shrugged. 'You can tell. Something about the feeling of the place.'

The terror swept over Charlie again. So Tracey had picked up an atmosphere too, had she?

'I don't *like* the feeling of the place. Let's go, Trace, before there's trouble.'

Please, Trace, please, she was saying inside. But Tracey laughed.

'Relax, Charlie. Have an apple.'

Tracey turned to the pretty little tree nearby and picked a fat red and yellow apple off it. It was so juicy it spurted everywhere and Tracey, giggling, mopped herself up with a handkerchief.

'Gorgeous,' she gurgled.

Charlie didn't like this at all. She'd an idea you

couldn't get into trouble for trespassing if you didn't do any damage and here was Tracey helping herself to fruit. But it wasn't that that was making her scared, no, it was something more than that. She got out a packet of gum and started on it to drive away the feeling.

'Let's find Jeff, shall we?' said Tracey, wandering up the garden path.

Charlie followed her moodily, not wanting to.

Chapter Eight

'What are we gonna do if someone finds us?' asked Charlie.

'Ask permission to look for the ball, of course,' answered Jeff, still rooting around in the bushes. Vince took no notice at all, being occupied with examining yet another creepy crawlie with his magnifying glass. Despair filled Charlie. She couldn't seem to get through to the other three at all. They were totally unbothered. Morons, she thought.

'Oh, you . . .' she began, but Tracey interrupted.

'Take no notice. She's just a wet blanket. Here, have an apple.'

She handed one to Jeff, who left off searching to eat it. Tracey was on her third, as if she couldn't get enough of them.

'Hey, don't leave me out,' cried Vince. 'What have I done?' So she gave one to him, but after taking a bite he threw it down, grimacing, yuck.

'Keep your rotten health food. I'd rather have chocolate.'

And he reached in his pocket for the supplies he always kept there.

'That was great,' murmured Tracey, who seemed to grow sunnier and happier by the minute. She ran across the lawn to a bush covered with glowing red flowers, picked one of them and pushed it into her hair, offered another to Charlie who crossly shook her head, turning away, then handed one to Jeff, who grinned and stuck it behind his ear.

'For you, Jeff, anything,' she laughed.

Charlie watched, feeling totally fed up. All she needed was Jeff and Tracey making goo-goo eyes at each other. For two pins she'd walk out of the place on her own. But even as she moved off to do this, fear crept up on her again, turning her inside to jelly, and she dared not leave the others.

'What a smashing place,' said Tracey. 'I feel great.'

She turned and danced on the lawn. After a moment Jeff did the same, pretending at first that he was sending her up but then dancing genuinely like Tracey. Vince rolled up his eyes in mock horror, grinning at Charlie.

'Gone bananas, the pair of 'em.'

Charlie didn't answer. She was listening for something, she didn't know what, or why. Everything was quiet except for Tracey humming her dance song. No birds, no traffic, no planes, no nothing, thought Charlie. And soon there will be no us. She began to shake again.

'It's waiting for us,' she managed to say to Vince, but he didn't seem to hear.

Tracey and Jeff flopped down on to the lawn, their faces pink, eyes shining. Tracey glowed like the red flower in her hair. After a minute she pointed towards the house.

'Vince, look at that fabulous butterfly!'

'Where?'

'Over there. Look. Look. There.'

'I still can't see it.'

'Neither can I,' muttered Charlie.

'Oh, come on, follow me. It's on those flowers. There. See.'

She jumped up, then tiptoed towards the house, followed by Vince. Jeff followed and so did Charlie, scowling horribly.

'Stupid butterfly,' she growled. 'I wanna go. *Now.*'

Chapter Nine

High up in his eyrie Mr Magus was stirring in his chair as the black cat sat up on his lap.

'Some of them have taken the bait, Gib,' whispered the old man.

The black cat purred loudly.

Chapter Ten

The four of them stood staring at the window surrounded by pots of blossoming flowers. One of the two large panes of glass was broken, cracks radiating from a round hole in the centre. They stood still, looking at it, Vince hanging back, Charlie drawing apple patterns in some dust with her racers, Tracey and Jeff still eating fruit and wearing flowers in their hair. It was very quiet. At last Jeff spoke.

'So that's where it went. Funny. I didn't hear any breaking glass. Let's go in.'

He knew the ball must be somewhere inside.

But Charlie cried out loudly, 'No, it's wrong. Let's get the heck out of here.'

The others looked in surprise, Jeff annoyed. Who did she think he was? Jeff Stanner never gave up easily.

'Not without that ball.'

He turned to Vince, skulking behind Charlie.

'Come on, Vince.'

Tracey's nose was squashed against the cracked window, as she peered inside, liking what she saw in there.

'Oh, wow! Can you get us in, Jeff?'

'Piece of cake.'

He slid his hand carefully through the jagged hole, slipping the lock from the inside, then drew out his hand again. The door slid open easily, silently.

'Fantastic,' said Tracey, looking at him as if he were a film star cum pop star rolled into one. 'Coming, Charlie?'

'Not me,' said Charlie, drawing back.

'Coming, Vince?' and as Vince hesitated, he added, 'I'm only getting the ball. It's gotter be somewhere here.'

But Vince's face had gone sulky, pushing out his bottom lip.

'No.'

'Chicken!' sneered Jeff, then laughed as he stepped into the room, Tracey right on his heels.

Vince glared at them and turned away towards Charlie, still drawing apples in the dust, looking dead miserable. Together they both started to hurry back down the garden.

'I'm not really chicken,' explained Vince. 'I just want to go home.'

'Me, too.'

They followed the winding path through the trees and the bushes. It seemed narrower than Charlie remembered, more overgrown and branches caught at them as they went. Somehow it didn't look beautiful to her at all. She couldn't remember why she'd thought it was when they first climbed over the fence.

'A horrible place,' she shivered.

And on they went, almost running now, but the fence seemed to be further away than they remembered. The garden was growing longer like walking on an endlessly moving belt as they tried to reach the end of it. Panic once more grabbed Charlie. The hair on the back of her neck prickled. She looked round nervously.

'I know we're being watched. Let's get a move on.'

Chapter Eleven

Mr Magus stopped stroking the black cat and gave him a slight push.

'Go, Gib, go,' he said.

The door opened a fraction as the cat jumped from the old man's lap and slipped round the edge of it and out of the room.

Chapter Twelve

'It's very grand,' Tracey said softly.

'The ball must be somewhere in here,' answered Jeff, going on to his hands and knees to peer under a sofa, and then under the chairs. Tracey wandered round looking at the pictures, picked up the piano lid and ran her fingers over the keys. The notes rang sweetly and she hummed a little, feeling not at all strange about being in someone else's house. It was as if she had been there before, had in fact, always known it.

'I must have been here at some time,' she said to Jeff, 'perhaps when I was very little so that I'd forgotten it, but it's come back now. It's a smashing place, isn't it?'

'Mm. Is that it? Behind the bookcase?'

Silly old Jeff. Rabbiting on about his stupid football. Bit of a wally, really. But very nice and quite dishy, not as deadly as he used to be.

'No, I can't see it. Hey, there's some smashing kids' books here, though. Charlie'd love 'em. Pity she went off like that. In one of her moods, I guess. Here's that one she's always reading, but it's in hardback. Looks quite posh. Not like old Charlie's tatty paperback.'

She curled up on the sofa with the book and leafed through it, while Jeff went on searching. One of the pictures caught his eye.

'See this, Trace?'

She nodded. 'Yes, it's an old man with a cat on his lap. I think he owns the house. I know him from somewhere. Oooh, I could go to sleep.'

'Thought any more about what I said earlier, Trace?'
'Wha'?'
'About coming out with me, Trace?'
She closed her eyes.
'Dunno. Might think about it. Oh, it's so nice here.'
Jeff took off his sunglasses and was about to sit down by her. Then he went on searching round the room for the ball instead. He just couldn't stop. Which was strange for he didn't care whether he found it or not.

Charlie and Vince had reached the garden fence at last. It appeared to have taken them ages, and Charlie had been terrified when she once more came across the pond and the stone cat with the eyes that watched. Then they landed in a bed of stinging nettles that they couldn't remember at all and that didn't seem to fit the garden. But they skirted round them until the fence appeared just in front of them. Loomed just in front of them. Suddenly. And loomed was the word.
'I'll get stuck. It's higher this time,' complained Vince, looking up at it.
It was. Much. Vince's stomach dropped into his feet. He was scared stiff of climbing, terrified of heights. This didn't even look like the same fence and he hadn't liked getting over it earlier, only Jeff had urged him on, pushing and shoving.
'I'll help you,' said Charlie, don't mess about, she added inside. 'Only come on. Before . . .'
'Before what?'
'I dunno.' She didn't even dare think about it, let alone mention the fear inside her. All she could do was to escape as far away as possible. 'Come on, Vince.'
(She was quaking. Vince too was afraid, but his fears were not Charlie's.)
She hauled herself up quite easily, being little and

light. There, she'd made it. And on the other side of the fence she could see Millington Park, dear ordinary Millington Park. Nearly as familiar as home. Once down on the other side of the fence she would be safe. Everything would be fine. She'd been imagining things. Just a touch of sun (though there wasn't any sun).

Vince was still standing in the garden, looking up at her.

'I'm losing me bottle. Bunk me up.'

'No, I'm not going back in there again,' cried Charlie. 'Take my hand and I'll pull! Now . . .'

And from out of nowhere a screeching, clawing black cloud leapt at Charlie, knocking her off the fence so that she fell and rolled, screaming, back into the garden and on top of Vince.

'That cat. That horrible monster cat,' sobbed Charlie.

Vince struggled to his feet, bewildered, shaking his head, suddenly too big for him.

'I dunno. I didn't even see it.'

Charlie shook with fear and fury. 'I knew something would stop us. I knew it.'

Vince couldn't face the fence again. It looked like the North Face of the Eiger to him. He wanted Jeff to sort things out.

'Let's get the others,' he said.

Panicking, they ran up the garden to the house and the broken window. This time it didn't seem far and nothing hindered them.

'Jeff, Jeff,' called Vince.

'Tracey!'

Totally relaxed, Jeff strolled to the window.

'You've decided to join us after all. Come on in. Don't mess about,' he added as they hesitated. Vince entered, with Charlie following slowly behind.

Tracey was curled up on the sofa.

'Hey, what got you? Run into Frankenstein?'

'No, Frankenstein's monster cat!' sniffled Charlie, half laughing, half in tears. 'It stopped us getting away.'

Tracey raised her eyebrows.

'What monster cat? You're imagining things.'

And at that moment the cat walked into the room, slipped past Charlie and went out through the door that was ajar.

'There! I told you.'

'What, that? That's just an ordinary little cat,' drawled Jeff.

Chapter Thirteen

Charlie grabbed Tracey and tried to pull her off the sofa.

'We're getting out of here *now*.'

Tracey shrugged her off, quite gently.

'Why? I like it here. There's no hurry.'

Charlie waved her hands in the air, her face wild.

'Can't you see? There's something terribly wrong with this house. And that cat.'

Tracey sighed. 'It's just a cat, Caroline.' Her voice was very polite and tedious, as if Charlie were some naughty toddler. Charlie stared at her in something like horror.

'Caroline? Caroline? You flipped or somethin'? Caroline? Nobody ever calls me that.'

It was true. People even forgot her real name, or thought it must be Charlotte. But it was Caroline Maria. She'd settled on Charlie when she was about four and made everybody else do the same simply by screaming her head off whenever they called her Caroline. She was too old to do that now, though she felt like it, standing in that room with Tracey lying there like the Queen Bee and pretending to be grand, and speaking in a very refined voice.

'Such a pretty name. I like things to be pretty and nice. Look at those lovely flowers. They're charming, all those lilies and roses.'

She waved a hand at the lilies and roses and ferns she could see arranged all over the room.

'Charming?' This wasn't a word Charlie ever used.

Nor did the flowers look like lilies and roses to her.

'Charming? Those things? They'd eat you for breakfast and spit out the pips.'

She'd never seen such horrible bunches of cruel-looking plants.

'I wish you wouldn't talk like that. Girls should talk nicely.'

Charlie peered closely into her face to see if Tracey was having her on, if it was all a game she was playing, she hoped. Please, she thought, any minute it'll be all right, it'll just be silly old Trace again and we can all go home. But Tracey stared back perfectly seriously.

'I don't believe it. Charming! Nicely!' Charlie muttered.

'I say, Vince, look at this,' called out Jeff. They were both exploring the room.

'Wha'?'

'A super butterfly collection.'

Vince waddled over. He had been feeling sleepy but at these words he woke up.

'Hey, it's fab!'

And it was. A wave of excitement swept through him, which he wanted to share.

Charlie came over, her face closed in, moody. She wouldn't look in the cabinet.

'No way. I bet they're all deformed or mutilated,' which made Vince angry.

'What deya mean, stupid nutter?'

It was only what they used to call one another but it upset Charlie.

'There. You said it. Let's go. Before they stick us on pins marked SPECIMENS ABCD. Dead Stupid Nutters.'

Jeff frowned.

'I don't understand what you're saying, Caroline.'
'Oh no, Jeff! Not you as well!' cried Charlie.

They stared angrily at each other over the butterfly cabinet, about to have a first class row, but at that moment Tracey got off the sofa and drifted over to the door as if she were in a school play, playing Lady of the Manor.

'Are you coming, everybody? It's time to go, Jeffrey, Vincent, Caroline.'

It's a wonder she doesn't add come along children, thought Charlie, but even more strongly came the thought that they mustn't go any further into the house – if they went anywhere it must be out, not in. She ran to get between Tracey and the door.

'Please, Tracey, don't go!'

And then she noticed what looked like the back of a picture that had been turned to the wall.

'What's that?' she asked, pointing at it.

Boss Jeff spoke. 'It's only the back of a picture. No need for alarm, Caroline.'

He reached up to it.

'Don't turn it round,' cried Charlie, then as if to explain herself, 'You don't know . . . what we'll see.'

'It's a mirror. Just as I thought, Caroline,' said Jeff, sounding incredibly stuck-up and superior.

'Don't-call-me-Caroline,' she gritted through her teeth.

'Honestly, it's all right. Everything's ready for us children. Excuse me, Caroline,' said Tracey, still talking as if Charlie were about three and retarded with it, so Charlie moved aside helplessly as Tracey opened the door, and sailed through, with first Jeff and then Vince following her.

Charlie felt bewildered.

'What's all ready for us? Tracey? Jeff? Vince?'

They didn't answer, so after a minute and looking round the room which gave her the creeps, she followed after them. From next door could be heard the sound of voices, so she followed, since above all else she didn't want to be left alone. For, she muttered to herself, who knew what might ooze out of the woodwork after her, and she wasn't sure she was as brave as Sandy any more. Though Sandy only had a crumbling cave to cope with, not a crazy house and friends that changed into something different as they talked.

The black cat she tried not to think about. *That* was the most frightening of all.

Next door was the kitchen, and for a minute Charlie felt a sense of relief, for it was a homely, friendly place. There was a spread too, all along the work-tops food was laid out: snacks, sausages, crisps, nuts, sandwiches, doughnuts, hot baked potatoes, beefburgers, coke, orangeade, yoghourt, soft-coloured drinks in bottles with straws, and everywhere fruit, apples, plums, pears, peaches, melons, damsons, strawberries and others Charlie didn't recognize.

Her friends were smiling at her, pleased that she'd joined them.

But what hit Charlie in the eye more than anything else was a huge poster pinned on the wall, with beautiful lettering in black and red and gold. It read:

WELCOME

TO TRACEY AND CAROLINE,
JEFFREY AND VINCENT.
MR MAGUS IS WAITING FOR YOU.

racey
roline
ffrey
cent
us is
ting
ou

Chapter Fourteen

Up in his eyrie Mr Magus talked to his black cat, Gib, who had sidled round the door into the room.

'Have they all arrived? Safely in one piece? We don't want them damaged, do we?'

The cat leapt on to his lap and was stroked.

'Are they . . . happy?'

The cat lifted its chin to have it rubbed. Mr Magus bent his head and appeared to listen to it.

'Oh, two of them are. The other two? Never mind. We'll help them. Then they'll be good. Children are good when they do what they should.'

The cat purred loudly.

Chapter Fifteen

Jeff, Tracey and Vince helped themselves to the food and drink, chattering cheerfully. Tracey turned on the radio and the sound of music filled the room.

'My favourite,' laughed Tracey. 'Marvellous.'

Charlie crouched on a stool, head down, hands tucked between her knees, looking even smaller and thinner than usual, withdrawn into herself. She was desperately afraid, afraid to stay, afraid to leave on her own. Jeff came over to her.

'Do try some of this, Caroline. It will make you feel better.'

Charlie shook her head and slumped even lower, the combination of that food and Jeff's new voice making her feel sick.

'Do cheer up. It's so lovely here,' Tracey said.

'How can I cheer up? We shouldn't be here. You shouldn't be here eating that . . . that stuff.'

'Why ever not?' asked Tracey in surprise.

'It's probably poisoned, that's why not . . . And anyway it's wrong to sit in someone's house eating their grub. Specially when they're not with you.'

'It says WELCOME to us with our names on it. It's been prepared specially for us,' said Jeff, annoyed.

'I don't understand any of this. But I do know welcome's what the Spider said to the Fly,' answered Charlie.

Vince was perched in his own corner of the kitchen with a heaped-up plateful of goodies, on which he tried to balance an extra doughnut. He was grinning happily at his collection but at Charlie's words his face changed. Doubt had crept in.

'Did I hear you say poison?'

He glared suspiciously at his plate.

'I'm not eating this.'

In a sudden temper he hurled the plate across the kitchen.

'I'm too fat, anyway. I know what. I'll start a new diet. Like not eating. Ever.'

Then he got out his matchbox and his magnifying glass to have yet another look at his insects.

'It's very bad manners to throw food about, Vincent,' said Tracey disapprovingly.

'Very naughty. You must pick it up,' added Boss Jeff.

Vince privately agreed with them, but telling him what to do started to make him stroppy.

'Get knotted!' he snapped back.

Jeff put down his own plate and stood up slowly and carefully.

'I don't wish to hear that sort of language here. Now get down and clean up the mess you've made.'

It was a jolly good imitation of their headteacher at Millington school. Vince couldn't believe it.

'You must be joking.'

Jeff moved over, menace written all over him, shoulders up, fists at the ready.

'I'm not in the habit of joking. Now are you going to pick it up willingly or shall I make you?'

Vince hadn't the courage to stand up to him.

'Oh, all right,' he agreed sulkily, then hissed, 'Pig,' under his breath. Sighing heavily, he bent down to pick up the food, now scattered over the kitchen tiles, plonked it on the plate and put that back on the work-surface. Jeff returned to his own food, piling another helping on his plate.

'This fruit is out of this world,' said Tracey. 'You really ought to try some, Caroline. You'd love it. I don't know what this one's called but it's absolutely delightful.'

Charlie jumped up.

'What's got into you two? Why are you talking like two old school teachers? Do you know something I don't?'

She'd got that feeling that something was going on behind her back, that she was missing out on a secret, being made a fool of.

'No,' said Jeff. 'Caroline, it's *you* that's strange today.'

'No, I'm not. *This* is.'

She pointed to the food, the cans of drink, the poster on the wall.

Jeff leaned over and whispered to Tracey:

'I'm afraid she's forgotten.'

This made Charlie even more uneasy. She wasn't at all sure whether there was something wrong with them or with her.

'Don't whisper about me! I'm not barmy.'

Jeff and Tracey looked at each other and slowly shook their heads.

'Never mind, dear. You're safe with us here.'

The thought that she had to depend on them and the house for safety made Charlie want to smash something, and that, funnily enough, brought back some of her usual fighting spirit.

'I wouldn't count on that.'

She decided to get to the bottom of all this, find out just what was going on. She got off her stool, whirled round and pointed at the Welcome poster.

'How did that thing get our names on it?'

Tracey selected a particularly large cream doughnut

oozing with jam and cream and licked it slowly, catching with her tongue the dollops of cream that oozed out of it.

'Mr Magus knows our names,' she said.

'And who's this Mr Magus when he's at home?'

Jeff sighed heavily.

'Now listen, Caroline –' he sounded just as if he was taking Assembly. 'He promised us a little party for helping him on the School's Age Concern Project. You must remember. Surely. You were with us.'

'Now *you* listen to me. We've never ever set foot in this house before. There's been no School Age Concern Project, 'cause we're on holiday. Right? We met in the park today. You kicked the ball and broke a window. We followed it. Right?'

She nearly added, And the Cat Sat on the Mat, but thought it might confuse things more than they were already.

Tracey frowned. 'Broke a window? What window? What ball?'

'Jeff's brother's ball. Jeff went on and on about it. Boringly. So we came to get it back. Into this house.' It was Charlie's turn to explain carefully. Tracey was looking at her in amazement.

So was Jeff. 'My brother's in the army,' he said. 'He doesn't play football. There isn't any ball.'

'We were invited properly. We certainly didn't break in,' Tracey squeaked with indignation.

'Who invited us?' asked Charlie.

'Mr Magus, of course. You can't have forgotten.'

'I've never ever heard of old Magus before.'

'Don't speak so rudely, Caroline. Jeffrey, I think we'd better go.'

'Yes,' Jeff said, in a voice like a robot's. 'Mr Magus is waiting for us.'

Tracey stood up, smiling. That smile alarmed Charlie even more. She turned to Vince but he was having a sulky fit and wouldn't look up.

'So we must go to him,' said Tracey, still smiling. 'Come along, Jeffrey. And you too, Vincent. Caroline, come along. Stop playing about.'

This was too much.

'You've gone stark raving bonkers,' cried Charlie in despair.

'Nutters, you mean,' grunted Vince in the background.

Chapter Sixteen

'They are nearly here, Gib, my cat. They enjoyed our welcome, didn't they? The little feast.'

The cat's purrs filled the room.

'I'm glad they have come. It's lonely to be old. I'll whisper it for your ears only, Gib, my cat, but I am so very weary of the world and of waiting. And the children have come to lift our burden. So young, so strong. They will help us, Gib.'

Chapter Seventeen

Charlie ran to Vince, still sulking in his corner.

'Vince, Vince. *You* remember the ball and the broken window. Tell *them*.'

Vince turned away from her. 'I dunno, Charlie. It's all muddled and I can't think straight.' He clutched at his stomach. 'You don't think that food was poisoned, do you? I ate a bit of roll and I don't feel too good.'

Charlie wasn't much bothered about his not feeling too good. She wanted to make sure she wasn't going barmy.

'Look, you've got to remember. Comon. You've got to help. Think of that horrible cat!'

Even as she thought of the cat fear grabbed her even more strongly. Which was strange for Charlie liked cats, all animals in fact, but then this was no ordinary cat. Vince puzzled in his head as he tried to remember a cat but he was feeling woollier and woollier, and the more he puzzled the worse it got. Being Vince, he gave up the struggle.

'Wha'? We don't want any trouble, Charlie.'

Charlie looked into Vince's blank and wandering eyes. There was no help or support there.

'You hopeless git!' she growled in a burst of sudden anger.

Jeff and Tracey had moved into a large light pleasant hall. Above an old polished chest hung a picture or a mirror turned to the wall. Near the stairs a door stood half open. Tracey looked in. She loved this house with its spacious rooms, its big stairway and mysterious atmosphere. She'd like to live here instead of being stuck with her mother and sister in their tiny rabbit hutch of a flat. For this house was a place where things could happen, parties, adventures, secrets, romance, a house for films and television.

'Oh, Jeffrey, it's beautiful. It's a conservatory.'

Jeff looked blank.

'Look, all those wonderful plants. I've never seen anything like them before.'

Jeffrey nodded politely as he peered round the door.

'Yes, it's amazing.' He spoke in his new voice. 'And what interesting animal pictures. But we mustn't stay here.'

It was extremely important that they went up to the top of the house. Jeff could feel something pulling at him, urging him on. Something momentous was about to happen there and they mustn't be late.

'No, we mustn't be late. Mr Magus is waiting for us.'

That was it. Mr Magus was waiting for them. He had to go there with Tracey. He looked at Tracey. The old Jeff would have said he thought she was smashing. The new one said politely,

'I do like you very much indeed, Tracey.'

She smiled. Very gently. Quite different from the usual Tracey, not noted for being either kind or gentle.

'Do you?'

'Yes,' said Jeff, reaching out for her hand, feeling so warm, so happy, he wished that time could stand still there and then – except, of course, that they must go up to the top of the house to meet Mr Magus.

'I like you too, Jeffrey. You seem much nicer today.'

He wasn't at all like that nasty boy he used to be. Everything had grown very clear to her, in fact. Jeffrey

was the boy-friend she had been looking for – astonishing that he'd been there all the time really, but then, he'd changed so much it wasn't really like the same person. And best of all, Mr Magus was waiting for them.

Up the stairs they went, hand in hand, smiling serenely.

Vince and Charlie were not smiling serenely as they entered the hall a minute or two later. Charlie wore a ferocious scowl as a mask against any danger and Vince was holding his stomach, which seemed to be leading a life of its own. Charlie lifted up the object hanging turned to the wall to check if it was what she suspected.

'Yeah, I knew it,' she said.

'Wha'?' asked Vince. He really felt horrible.

'We're in the house of the Back to Front mirrors,' she answered. 'Why?'

'I dunno,' said Vince, true enough, he didn't know anything, except that he wanted a hole to crawl into and cover himself with leaves and wait till everything had gone away.

'Well, it's not us going through the Looking Glass, that's for sure.'

Vince didn't answer. He didn't really know what she meant anyway.

'I almost wish it was. This place scares me silly,' said Charlie.

She caught hold of the conservatory door. And looked in just as Jeff and Tracey had done. And wished she hadn't.

'Oh, no, no, no, no,' she wailed. 'Oh, how horrible.'

The anguish in her voice was enough to stir even Vince.

'What's up?'

'Can't you see? All those little dead animals. Mice and squirrels, birds, hanging on string. How cruel.'

Vince rubbed his eyes. 'It's all misty.'

'More scary plants as well,' Charlie moaned. 'Insect-eating plants. Oh, this horrible house.'

'Come away from there.'

Vince dragged her away from the doorway.

Chapter Eighteen

The cat was waiting for Jeff and Tracey as they arrived hand in hand at the top of the house. They turned to one another and smiled.

'We're here,' said Jeff.

'At last,' Tracey answered.

'The nice pussy cat has come to fetch us,' said Jeff, going to stroke it but then changing his mind. Gib was not a cat to be stroked easily.

'Shall we wait for the others?' asked Tracey.

'I'll call them.' Jeff leaned over the banisters. 'Vincent! Caroline!'

Impatiently the cat pushed through the doorway and then turned and looked at them. They were obviously expected to follow. Still smiling, still hand in hand, Jeff and Tracey entered the room, Mr Magus's eyrie.

Charlie and Vince had arrived on the first landing, where a partly opened door showed a bathroom.

'I'm going in there,' announced Charlie.

'OK,' replied Vince, not caring one way or another. He waited, bored, rubbing his eyes and nursing his stomach, a picture of misery.

'I was right,' said Charlie, emerging. 'There are no mirrors in there at all. No mirrors in a bathroom, Vince? It's crazy.'

'What's she rabbiting on about?' wondered Vince.

Not that he cared, anyway.

'I feel rotten. I can't see and I've got bellyache. I

wanna go home, Charlie.'

Charlie wanted to go home, too. More than anything else. But then she heard their names.

'Listen! That's Jeff calling us. We can't really go on without them, can we?'

She went on to the next flight of stairs, Vince miserably in tow. At the top of the house were three doors, one of them partly open. For the cat, thought Charlie, these open doors are for that cat. And at the thought of him all she wanted to do was to rush out of the place and put the greatest possible distance between her and it. But she was sure that Jeff and Tracey were in there, and as well as feeling afraid she was also . . . curious. Perhaps now, she'd find out what this was all about, the billion dollar question, Who is Mr Magus? She stood for a moment outside the partly opened door.

Behind her Vince groaned.

'They must be in here,' said Charlie.

'I'm off,' came from behind.

Charlie swung round, 'No you're not. You're staying.'

She grabbed him as he tried to cut and run.

And at that moment the cat slipped through the door, looking small and neat. It twined itself round Charlie's legs, rubbing her affectionately. She looked at it in disbelief.

'I don't believe it. That's not the same cat.'

It pushed the door further open with its head and a voice spoke.

'Come in,' said Mr Magus.

Tracey and Vince were seated on the floor at the feet of a very old man in a leather armchair. His long silky beard flowed down to his knees. They gazed at him as if they had known and loved him for a long, long time. The cat leapt on to his lap and settled among the beard, purring and kneading with its paws. At first glance it seemed to Charlie a picture of peace and contentment. Until the old man turned his penetrating blue eyes on her. Those eyes had known and seen many things. Charlie turned her own away.

Vince saw none of this. He was lost in an aching mist with a sharp centre of pain and misery at the middle. Perhaps he would wake up soon and find it was all a nightmare caused by a takeaway gulped down too quickly at supper time.

The old man motioned them to sit on the floor beside the others. Vince turned bewildered to Charlie who pulled him down beside her, none too gently. She couldn't really forgive Vince for being not with anything just when she needed him.

'Now we are all here,' said the old man. 'My name is Mr Magus. Welcome to my world, children.'

'Thank you, Mr Magus,' chorused Jeff and Tracey.

Vince and Charlie mumbled. Charlie didn't know what to say and Vince felt too ill to care.

'You enjoyed the little feast?'

'Very much indeed, sir,' said Jeff.

'Delicious,' smiled Tracey.

Once more there were mumbling noises from the other two. Mr Magus appeared to find it all satisfactory for he smiled and said:

'Good. You need to eat well for a full and happy life. Meet Gib, my cat. But then, you've already met, haven't you, Caroline?'

Charlie felt the edge of fear at the mention of the cat. Despite its harmless appearance at the door she was still afraid of it. She switched her attention to the contents of the room, the pictures on the wall, noticing that one was turned round, not facing them. It's bound to be a mirror, she thought, and then saw the globe and the astrolabe and other strange objects.

Tracey and Jeff were still gazing adoringly at Mr Magus. He spoke softly to them.

'I wanted you to come,' he said. 'We need you, Gib and I.'

'We'd do anything for you, Mr Magus,' said Tracey in a low voice.

'Yes, sir,' agreed Jeff.

Brainwashing, Charlie's mind clicked suddenly. That's it. They've been brainwashed, the pair of 'em.

'Oh, it's wonderful to have you happy and contented here with me!' Mr Magus smiled benignly over his little flock. I can't stand this, thought Charlie. I've got to do something. Here we go.

'Mr Magus,' she asked.

'Caroline?'

'Jeff and Tracey say I've been here before. But I haven't. And they say I've met you before. It's not true.'

Mr Magus's smile was dark and inscrutable.

'Your mind is cloudy, Caroline, so that you can't see things clearly.'

'No, that's Vince, not me.'

She wasn't going to be led off the point with a lot of old blah.

'How did you know our names?'

Vince clutched his stomach as a specially fierce pang caught him. His eyes were shut tight.

'Perhaps you're too young to understand,' said Mr Magus.

'Grown-ups say that when they don't want you to understand,' said Charlie. 'How did you know our names?'

She was determined to get a reasonable answer.

He looked away, way out beyond the waving tree-tops beneath the window.

'I know many things – your names among them.'

'He's so clever,' sighed Tracey.

'So wise,' added Jeff.

It was all too much.

'So fiddlesticks,' shouted Charlie, jumping up. 'It's a trick!'

Chapter Nineteen

She ran to Jeff and Tracey and shook them by their shoulders.

'Wake up. You're zonked out,' she told them.

Jeff was furious, pushing away her hands in disgust. So did Tracey.

'I wish you'd behave properly.'

'She was always the same,' put in Tracey. 'Remember that school trip? She got us all into trouble then.'

Charlie turned to Mr Magus, not caring how old or terrifying he might be. Or wise or clever.

'What have you done to them?'

'Perhaps I have opened their eyes a little.'

Tracey's eyes were filled with dreams. 'I'm going to be rich and beautiful,' she murmured, and she smiled as she thought of it all.

Jeff sat up very straight. 'Great things,' he said, in a deep, sonorous voice, 'can be achieved by those under control. Fame. Power.'

'I don't believe it,' cried Charlie. 'You can't mean all this!'

'You must believe me,' said Jeff. 'Listen. Here's an example. Already, Tracey likes me and she didn't before. She's *my* girl now.'

'Is that true?' Charlie asked Tracey, remembering some of the things she'd said about him that very day.

'Oh, yes,' smiled Tracey. 'Thanks to Mr Magus.'

'You sound like a commercial. I must be going crazy,' cried Charlie.

'But you are crazy. That's always been your trouble,' answered Jeff.

'Too much imagination. All that reading,' echoed Tracey.

Vince's misery was growing stronger and stronger till he almost felt he could bear no more. Poison, it must have been poison, he thought in despair. Then he lurched to his feet, greener than wet grass in spring.

'What's the matter, child?' asked Mr Magus.

'I'm gonna be sick,' Vince just managed to say before he fled to the bathroom.

A few minutes later he stood alone on the landing outside the bathroom, pale but reviving. Vince was almost his own horrible self once more. 'That's better. I can see properly again. Got rid of that bloomin' poison stuff. Must have lost some weight.

He looked round.

'Charlie's right. It is creepy here. I've half a mind to get the heck out of it. Yet that batty old geezer seems harmless enough. And the others'll be mad at me if I do scarper. I'll go back and see if there's anything in this for me.

'But I'm keeping the old lamps skinned. Any trouble with old Magus Fagus and old Vince is up and away.'

He trotted back up the stairs to the others. They were still there, Tracey and Jeff holding hands.

'Are you better now, Vincent?' asked Mr Magus.

I'm playing this by ear, thought Vince.

'Yes,' he smiled and nodded. 'Thank you. Much better. I'm ready to listen to you, Mr Magus.'

'Good boy,' smiled the old man.

Mr Magus turned to Charlie, whose thoughts ran round in her head like mice on a cage-wheel.

'Why don't you relax and be happy too? Here in this

room, high above the world, you are safe.'

'Beautiful and safe,' murmured Tracey dreamily.

'I shall take care of you,' said Mr Magus, gently. Gib's purring re-echoed through the room. Charlie felt as if she were being rocked in a hammock high in some tree. Perhaps she was wrong and Tracey and Jeff right, perhaps Mr Magus was a wonderful, kind old man . . .

. . . she remembered the little animals strung up in the room below . . . No, she wasn't wrong. Mr Magus was no kind, gentle old man. She wasn't even sure what he was . . .

'I *want* to know what you *want*,' she said.

'To make you all happy,' he said, still gently.

'You keep saying that. Going home would make me happy.'

He wasn't angry.

'But of course, you can go home,' he smiled in the recesses of his beard. 'And back to school.'

'I can do without that,' muttered Vince.

'Cheerio, then,' grinned Charlie, standing up. 'I'm off.'

He sat more firmly upright in the leather chair.

'One moment,' he said, lifting a finger.

'I knew it,' Charlie said. 'What's the catch?' for she was by now convinced that he intended to keep them there.

The eyes turned on her, concentrating on her, reminded her of the eyes of a falcon in a wildlife poster she'd put up in her bedroom.

'There's no catch. Just put yourself under my control. Then all that is wicked in you will melt away. You'll return home with a changed personality . . .'

Charlie didn't care for the sound of that at all. She didn't think her personality was anything special but it was hers and she didn't want it messed about with by

some old boy looking like Old Father Time without the scythe.

'Whatjer mean by that?'

Tracey frowned and shook her head. Jeff looked down his nose at her.

'You'll be gentler, quieter. But you'll also be able to achieve whatever you want . . .'

'Two thousand bars of chocolate?'

'No, child, you joke,' he said, softly and seriously. 'I mean important things. Tracey wants to be beautiful.'

Tracey smiled and stretched out her arms. She saw herself on a huge screen, watched by admiring millions. 'Jeffrey wants to be great and powerful.'

Jeff took the salute as hundreds of armed men marched past.

'You – what do you want deep inside? Let me guess. I know. The cleverest of them all, Caroline? Would that be it?'

She wasn't going to let him know how near the mark he'd got.

Attack's the best form of defence, her Dad had always told her.

'What's in it for you?'

'Gib and I will grow young again. And you will, dear children, be part of me as I am part of you.'

This frightened Charlie more than anything yet.

'No way,' she cried. 'You're not gonna make me into a zombie! Like them.'

She pointed at Jeff and Tracey, who looked as if they were in some kind of trance, smiling into the distance and holding each other's hands.

'Tracey and Jeffrey are happy,' said Mr Magus.

'So are cabbages. And thanks all the same for that kind offer, but I don't want any part of you, Mr Magus. Nor that cat!'

Chapter Twenty

While Mr Magus had been talking to Charlie, Vince had been sitting up and taking notice, feeling fine, all his senses working at full revs. This set-up he found most peculiar, very shifty indeed, but with any luck there might be something in it for him.

'Mr Magus?' he asked.

'Yes, Vincent?'

'What will you give me?'

'What do you mean?'

Vince thought hard. If he could have anything he wanted, he'd settle for one thing and that would look after the rest.

'Lolly? Bread? Loot? Money?'

'That's not so easy. The only way you'll get money is by being dishonest, Vincent, and all that will be taken away from you. You'll be good, you see. That's the trouble.'

Vince lost interest.

'Don't think I want all this goodness stuff. Sounds dead boring to me. If I can't have money, then what about knowing what makes people tick and things work? I'll manage all right.'

'That could be done.'

'I tell you what I could fancy right now, a coke or some fruit or something. Can I go down to the kitchen and help myself?'

'A good idea. Tracey, you go with him to see he's all right.'

'I don't want to leave you,' protested Tracey.

The room was so loving, so comfortable, and she felt so safe there with Mr Magus and her new boy-friend, Jeff, that she was reluctant to leave it. But what Mr Magus told her to do, she must do, so she got up obediently.

'It's only for a minute, my dear,' said Mr Magus.

Tracey whispered into Jeff's ear, then went slowly out of the room with Vince.

Mr Magus turned back to Charlie. While he had been talking to Vince her brain had been racing round its computer circuits and arrived at a conclusion. She knew he would try to win her over and she waited.

'The others are all with me, Caroline. So why fight me? I'm stronger than you.'

The eyes glinted. Charlie looked away.

'I know,' she said quietly.

Jeff leaned forward eagerly. 'Stop arguing and be friends, Caroline. Please.'

'Did you say I'd be the cleverest?' asked Charlie.

'If you want to be.'

'In and out of school?'

'Both,' smiled Mr Magus.

Charlie sat and considered this. With great care.

'All right, Mr Magus,' she announced at last. 'I'm with you. Oh, you can call me Caroline if you want to.'

She smiled a wide innocent smile. Mr Magus smiled back.

'I'm delighted, Caroline,' he said.

Tracey and Vince made their way downstairs, Tracey dreaming of the future, seeing herself adored by millions, voted the most beautiful woman in the world for the third year running. With her stood Jeff, President of somewhere or other, she wasn't sure where (Tracey had never been any good at Geography), as great and powerful as she was beautiful. It was a good job that Charlie couldn't read her mind just then.

Vince wasn't dreaming of the future. He was just busy thinking up Ways of Escape. Part of him wished to cut and run on his own, but another part insisted the four of them must stick together.

Funny it was Charlie, he thought, who had sussed out danger first. Must be more to her than just being a stick insect. Still, the first and main thing was to convince Tracey that they had to get away from that grisly old boy that she'd taken such a shine to (along with taking a fancy to Jeff). Crazy. Just crazy.

When they arrived in the hall Vince said:

'Listen to me. That old geezer is completely round the twist.'

Tracey was jolted out of her daydream, picturing the evening gown that she'd wear when she was presented to the Queen following her part in Film of the Year. Should it be white? Or black? Or pink? Or glittering sequins? Vince's voice jarred like a pneumatic drill on a sunny afternoon.

'I don't know what you mean,' she answered huffily in her new up-market voice.

'He's got us here for some no good reason. To do us in or something. Like you read about in the papers.'

Tracey looked at him in disgust. What a nasty, fat, common slob – (no, she wouldn't use the word 'slob') – boy he was.

'I won't listen to what you're saying!'

He pushed his fat face near to hers.

'You and I are gonna suss the way out of this place, then go and get the other two.'

Tracey stepped back. What was she doing here with him and all his crazy ideas? Oh yes, Mr Magus had told her to look after him, she remembered. She must do what she was told.

'You're supposed to be getting some fruit from the kitchen. Eat and then you'll see straight.'

'No way. That kind of seeing straight's as twisted as a corkscrew. No, I'm heading for where old Jeff let us in for this lot.'

Tracey was disgusted!

Fancy talking in this dreadful fashion. So disloyal. So treacherous. She couldn't put up with this.

'I'm going back to tell Mr Magus about you!'

Oh, the stupid git, thought Vince.

'No, you're not,' he snapped.

And grabbed her before she could run back up the stairs and into the eyrie.

Vince was heavier than Tracey but not as tall, and she was quite a strong girl. He tried to pull her back. She pushed him away, grabbing an ear, which hurt Vince terribly, so that a red haze swam before his eyes. Why was he getting such a horrible deal from life on this particular afternoon? He hadn't done anything. Mad, he pulled her hair sharply in return and both of them stumbled against the conservatory door, which swung wide open, so that Vince saw the little dead animals hanging there just as Charlie had said. He stood rooted to the spot, sickened.

'Yuck and double yuck. Charlie was right. Dead creatures everywhere. Look at that!'

All his anger against Tracey vanished. Like the animals, they would be victims too unless they could save themselves.

Tracey straightened herself out. She shouldn't have been caught in a scuffle like that. Mr Magus wouldn't like her to scrap and fight. Quite disgusting. And what was Vince saying? He'd got everything wrong, as usual.

'What are you talking about? It's beautiful in there. I saw it before. All those lovely . . .'

Somehow, something was wrong. The room didn't seem the same as it had been before. It was altering, changing even as she looked. She rubbed her eyes, filled with disturbing doubts.

'Lovely . . . aren't they? It's all right . . . isn't it?'

She rubbed her eyes again.

'It's gone blurred . . . misty . . .'

She didn't want to see what she was now seeing, more clearly with every moment.

'Oh, no . . . how awful . . . those little dead . . . there's a squirrel . . . hanging . . . and little mice . . .'

Tracey, a soft-hearted girl, couldn't bear it. Tears sprang to her eyes. She was lost, bewildered. What was happening to her?

'Your drug's wearing off,' said Vince.

What was he on about? She wasn't on drugs. Some kids were, but not her. She wasn't so stupid.

'What drug?'

'I think it was something in the fruit you and Jeff ate.'

There was a pause as Tracey registered what Vince was saying.

'Listen,' he went on. 'Trace, I think your Mr Magus is some sort of magician. The bad kind. You see, he changes things so that they deceive you. There really was a ball and a broken window, Trace. Believe me.'

'I do. Now,' she sighed.

Doubt having set in, Tracey was thinking hard, as the bright dream bubble of Tracey the Bright and Beautiful Star floated away and burst and she was left with what? Vince – telling unpleasant truths.

And perhaps worse. Dangerous truths. About a reality not boring but frightening . . .

'All you ever wanted,' said Vince.

'What?' asked Tracey.

'Read the headlines. Four children found dead in house of mad magician.'

It was too much. Tracey started to cry.

There was no sympathy from Vince. Except where Vince was concerned he was a hard case.

'Belt up,' he said.

And at that moment Charlie appeared.

'Hey, how did you get away from there?' Vince asked, jerking his thumb upwards in the direction of Mr Magus's eyrie.

'Fooled him. He thinks I'm after fruit. Like you. Which will make us into his yes men. He hopes. That fruit alters the way you see things.'

She looked at Tracey, who was still weeping.

'Trace? Are you OK?'

'She knows. She saw the room with the animals. That did it. Let's get out of here.'

He felt uneasy talking in the hall. That cat could be listening anywhere. Just to escape from this house was all he wanted.

'The room with the broken window. That's where we can get out,' he went on. 'Should be easy.'

'This way, then,' said Charlie. 'But we've got to get Jeff away as well.'

'First check our escape route,' Vince said. 'Come on.'

Tracey stopped crying and together they returned to the garden room, hurrying now, for they desperately wanted to return to safety and ordinariness.

'Here we are!' cried Charlie.

The window looked blankly back at them, not a hole or break anywhere, all the glass intact.

Bewildered, Tracey said, 'It isn't broken after all. But you said . . .'

To hide his fear, Vince snarled with anger.

'If it isn't broken, it soon will be,' he cried.

Charlie, cooler, had crossed the room and was trying to open the catch, but it wouldn't budge. Vince seized a statuette of a mermaid and banged it against the glass. But the mermaid broke, not the glass. He grabbed a chair and with a strength none of them knew he had, crashed it against the huge pane.

Nothing happened. The window was still intact. Vince dropped the chair in disgust.

'There's no way out of here!' he whispered, as Tracey and Charlie stared at each other.

Chapter Twenty-one

Upstairs in Mr Magus's room all was peaceful and still. Jeff sat dreaming of future power and glory, all sorts of possibilities unfolding before him – he could be a head-teacher, a general, a space pilot, he could rule the world; with the help of Mr Magus. All he had to do was to stay under his control. And Tracey, his girl, would walk beside him all the way. Those were Jeff's thoughts. What Mr Magus's thoughts were, who could say? At last Jeff stirred and spoke.

'They've been gone a long time, sir. Do you think they're all right?'

'They'll be back,' Mr Magus replied softly.

But Jeff was still bothered. Were his friends going to let him down? He wasn't at all sure they were up to Mr Magus's high standards. He started to explain.

'Caroline's strange. Unreliable, you know. And you can't trust Vince. He might nick – I mean steal, sir – some of your valuables. Do you think I should fetch them back?'

'If you wish, Jeffrey.'

'I think I ought to. See that they're behaving properly.'

He stood up, still talking,

'You know what I mean, sir. I think I ought to, sir. Excuse me, please.'

Mr Magus nodded and Jeff went out.

After a moment Mr Magus spoke to his cat.

'I think the children may be a little troublesome. Go, Gib, my cat.'

Gib stood up, stretched and slipped like a shadow through the partly opened door.

Jeff ran down the stairs to the hall to where the other three had retreated from the garden room, not knowing what to try next or where to go.

'What are we gonna do now?' asked Vince, just as Jeff joined them.

'Do? Why, go back upstairs, of course. Mr Magus is waiting for us.'

'Oh, not that again,' cried Charlie.

Then Jeff spotted Tracey's face (tear-stained). Her mascara had run and her hair was scruffed up. She looked terrible.

'What are you crying for?'

He looked indignantly at the other two.

'Have they been upsetting you?'

He could believe anything of Vince and Charlie.

'Jeff,' began Tracey, trying to explain to him and finding it very difficult.

'Call me Jeffrey, please.'

'No. Jeff.' She had to get *that* clear. Now for it. 'Mr Magus has been tricking us.'

'Rubbish,' replied Jeff.

'Oh, come on,' said Vince. 'You've been taken in. That man's up to something.'

Jeff felt absolutely fed up with them all. Hadn't they got any loyalty? But he must keep his temper, keep in control.

'You've got it all wrong,' he said patiently.

'The window's been mended and we can't get away,' Tracey said.

'Not this broken window stuff again!'

Honestly, they'd got minds like three-year-olds.

Thick, solid, thick. He tried again. Charlie was supposed to be fairly bright. He tried to get through to her.

'Charlie, I thought you'd come round to agreeing with Mr Magus.'

'No, I was pretending. Look, come with me, Jeff, if you don't believe that he's wicked.'

He turned to Tracey. His girl. She had to be on his side. Mr Magus's side.

'Tracey? Tracey. You're with me, aren't you?'

Tracey shook her head, her face sad.

'It's all different now, Jeff. Oh, Charlie'll show you. What he's really like.'

Chapter Twenty-two

Jeff was reluctant but Charlie pushed him towards the conservatory door. She'd got to make him see things as they were and then they could make their escape.

'Look in there,' she said.

'I've already seen it. Very nice. A conservatory.'

He wasn't interested. Just humouring old Charlie who everyone knew was crazy.

'I want to know what's up with Tracey.'

'Take another look. Please . . .'

He couldn't think why he'd thought Charlie was bright. She was really just stubborn.

'Don't be silly, Charlie. This is stupid.'

She practically pushed him into the room, so he had to look. Better get it over and then he could get them all back to Mr Magus *and* find out what was wrong with Tracey.

He looked. And rubbed his eyes.

'I can't see. It's all . . . misty.'

And then suddenly the mist cleared and Jeff could see properly.

'Oh, no . . .'

There was a long silence.

'. . . Charlie . . .'

Jeff hid his face.

Charlie said gently, 'You see?'

He still didn't speak. After a moment:

'Now do you believe me?' asked Charlie. For the first time in her life she felt really sorry for Jeff. She remembered how she'd felt the first time she'd seen it. And it was worse for Jeff, for he had believed in Mr Magus.

They were joined by Vince and Tracey. Tracey had done herself up a bit and looked something like her old self.

'He's seen the light, then?' asked Vince.

'Yeh. I think,' said Charlie.

'I'm sorry. Poor Jeff,' said Tracey.

Jeff looked up at last.

'I feel awful. He promised so much . . .'

He seemed about to cry, poor macho Jeff. The girls were full of sympathy.

Vince had no such feelings.

'Yeah, yeah. But don't hang about. Grandad up there'll soon be after us, I bet.'

'There must be other ways to get out,' said Charlie.

Vince was looking round the hall. He seemed to have taken over the Boss role.

'Tracey,' he said, 'we'll try the kitchen. Charlie, you and Jeff the front.'

But Charlie was staring at something behind the others, her eyes wide and alarmed.

'It's maybe too late. Look.'

Gib, grown larger and more malevolent, was sitting on the stairs watching them.

Charlie stood mesmerized, the others alarmed.

'The monster cat,' she whispered.

'Run for it,' shouted Boss Vince.

And as if he'd pulled a switch they scattered, Jeff and Charlie to the front door, Vince and Tracey to the kitchen. Some minutes later they were back in the hall. Gib had disappeared.

'It's bloomin' hopeless. We can't get out,' panted Vince, out of breath after the mad rush.

'He's put a force field round the house,' said Jeff

hopelessly.

'We're trapped,' said Tracey.

Jeff could see no way of escaping Mr Magus's power, partly because he'd been so completely under his spell.

'We'll have to beg him to let us go.'

Surely he would relent then. But Vince had no illusions about Mr Magus (or anything else).

'You must be joking. We're his meal ticket. Four juicy children – ripening nicely . . .'

'No, don't say that,' cried Tracey, terrified.

But Charlie's fighting spirit was aroused. Maybe because she'd been scared long before the others, she'd grown accustomed to living with the fear of Mr Magus.

'It looks like we'll have to fight him. On his own special territory. Up there in that room. We need a plan. Think, all of you.'

Vince shook his head.

'All I can think is, Aren't we the Nutters? Getting ourselves into this lot?'

'That's better than nothing if it means . . .'

'We stick together,' joined in Jeff, perking up at last.

'You're a fine one to say that,' put in Vince, stirring things.

Charlie wanted them all together – not quarrelling.

'Leave it. This is no time to get at each other.'

Tracey had been thinking, thinking hard.

'There is something – something in this house, something odd . . . peculiar . . .'

'It's all peculiar,' put in Vince.

'No, not that. Something. Not the food. Not the dead animals, ugh, not the window . . .'

'Mirrors,' cried Charlie. 'It's something to do with the back to front mirrors!'

And Gib, grown larger still, stalked out of the conservatory door and towards them as they watched in horror.

Vince spoke what they were all thinking.

'He's been at his grub! Yuck!'

They backed away from the cat and as they did he herded them back to the stairs.

'Oh, we are the Nutters,' cried Vince.

Each of them in turn tried to resist, but they dared not face up to the black cat, and slowly, slowly, he forced them back to the eyrie at the top of the house where Mr Magus was waiting for them.

Chapter Twenty-three

He sat in his leather armchair as if he could wait for ever. Gib leapt up and perched once more on his lap, purring and kneading.

'Welcome, dear children. Please sit down.'

The four looked at each other, then sat down on the floor. Under his breath Vince muttered:

'Are you sitting comfortably? Then he'll begin.'

But Mr Magus picked this up.

'Oh no, Vincent. We'll all begin. Won't we, Gib?'

Perhaps more than any of them Charlie feared the cat, and she didn't wish to look at it, but like the others she was drawn and held as the cat's eyes glowed larger and brighter, taking them over, leading them to where the past afternoon unrolled before them like a video replay – seeing themselves in the park –

Tracey and Charlie, Charlie reading her tatty old paperback, specs halfway down her nose, Tracey fiddling with her hair, her face, her Big Bag. Charlie put up a hand to her nose, but the specs were in her pocket. Tracey felt for the Big Bag, still beside her on the carpet.

Silently they watched as Jeff and Vince came into view, Jeff playing tricks with the football, Vince with his magnifying glass studying insects, the backchat and the comments leading up to Jeff kicking the ball over the fence into the garden . . .

'. . . the garden . . .' whispered Charlie on an indrawn breath, all of them enthralled as they saw Tracey on the swing, Charlie wandering unhappily, Jeff finding the broken window, entering, and Tracey following, Vince and Charlie running to join them, Jeff in his sunglasses showing off to Tracey . . .

What they did not see was the terrified attempt at escape by Charlie and Vince and the cat's leap at Charlie to throw her back into the garden.

But there stood the feast in all its mouth-watering splendour. And the notice on the wall . . .

WELCOME
MR MAGUS IS WAITING FOR YOU

Gib's eyes closed sleepily and they were back in the upstairs room once more.

'I've waited for you to come,' the old man was saying. 'It seemed a long time. We heard of you and you were the ones we wanted, with your foolish ways. I wanted to save you. And us.'

Tracey spoke in a sad voice.

'You made fools of us. And now you're keeping us prisoner!'

'You can't keep us here against our will,' added Jeff.

Vince spoke, his voice anything but sad or gentle.

'We know about people like *you*. But we're not feeble little kids, y'know.'

'I gave you a chance,' said Mr Magus. 'I offered you your dreams. Now give in to me before it's too late. *Give in to me.*'

'No,' shouted Charlie.

'Please, Mr Magus, let us go home,' said Tracey. She turned to Jeff.

'You don't really want to keep us here,' he said.

Vince's face had set into the stroppy look that his mother knew only too well.

'Yes, it's been nice to meet you but me Mum gets bothered if I'm late for tea.'

He got up to go.

'Stay where you are. I need you,' ordered Mr Magus, his eyes snapping, as Gib's opened wide, beginning to glow again.

'Oh, we're getting the truth now,' Vince said.

'I need your youth, your energy, to renew mine so that I can go on living! So stop fighting me. NOW!' cried the old man.

How could I ever have thought he was kind and good? thought Tracey, cowering down, lifting her arms to protect herself.

Gib the cat, grown larger, menacing as a witch's cat, seemed to loom over them like a great beast, his black mouth with its red tongue and sharp white dagger teeth opening, a giant cave.

Every terror Charlie ever had was to be there in that room with that cat: Sandy, her heroine of the cave, a million miles away.

'No, no. He's going to eat us,' she screamed.

As did Tracey.

Jeff rose to fight, though he had no more hope of stopping the cat with his fists than of stopping a volcano erupting.

'It's the end,' thought Charlie, 'of us all.'

'I need you,' cried Mr Magus, towering over them, his long fingers working in the air like a magician's, his arms moving, drawing power from the children so that they shrank into dolls, puppets smaller than Gib's enormous eyes, now grown as big as lamps, as huge as planets, as he and Mr Magus became one being, then split into two again, then merged into one once more.

He controlled them with his hands, tiny creatures wheeling in a hugeness that could only be space, while stars and comets and great ringed planets rushed past them in intricate patterns and ever-increasing speeds.

There was beauty too vast for them to appreciate, as strength drained away from them. Sick, dizzy and weak, all they could do was hold on.

All at once they were on a planet, and there walking towards them on an alien purple shore came Mr Magus, dressed in weird garments, with Gib beside him, the man and the animal and merging into one as they came nearer and nearer. Then at another time, another place, a green plain and stone temples and Mr Magus, in a white tunic walking towards them with Gib, who mingled then with Mr Magus. A high hill and Mr Magus . . . with Gib. A mountain top, a tent in the desert, a crowded street with overhanging houses, a frozen shore with icy wind blowing stinging snow and Mr Magus with Gib . . .

Mr Magus with Gib . . . Mr Magus with Gib . . . everywhere, at every time, and taking them over completely as he took over Gib. So that Charlie and Tracey, Jeff and Vince, funny, stupid, sometimes right, often wrong, would be no more, nothing, no thing, no, o . . .

'Oh,' thought Charlie. 'No, no, no, no.'

Her cry of protest caught an answer from the others, no, it can't, it mustn't happen to us . . .

'Help,' cried Charlie in her mind, and the echo caught Jeff and Tracey so that they too cried out for help.

And Vince, ole fat insect-loving Vince, cried out to Mr Magus:

'No, no, you're just a load of rubbish!'

Chapter Twenty-four

Everything held still.

They were back in the eyrie above the tree-tops with Mr Magus and Gib, two separate beings once more, standing over the children.

Who were still there. All four of them and not yet defeated. Because we're together, thought Charlie.

Mr Magus and the cat seemed smaller, diminished.

'Why, you're so evil,' said Jeff softly, as if he saw things really clearly at last.

'Nothing more than a . . .' added Tracey.

'He's weakening! Shucks to you, Mr Magus!'

The old man seemed to be shrinking before them, back into his leather armchair.

Then he rallied, crying out:

'I'm still too strong for you.'

Dark shadows gathered in the corners of the room, moving across the wall, surrounding them, closing them in, horrible shapes that were all wrong so that the children hid their eyes, afraid of what they might see. The shadows loomed larger, darker, nearer, and Mr Magus raised his hands to dominate them once more.

Jeff lurched forward, fists up, with Charlie behind him. If they were to be snuffed out at least they'd go fighting, not crying.

The specs fell out of Charlie's pocket and on to the floor, her granny specs, good companions of many reading hours. She grabbed them and plonked them on her nose, where they slid halfway down as usual.

A ray of sunlight caught them, and glinted on Mr Magus. The whole room took the light, the shadows grew pale and receded into the corners.

Everything shone clear as the glinting glasses for Charlie. Well, almost everything, so that hope flared up strongly for the first time on that dreadful afternoon, and with it a belief that they could all come out of it safely.

'That's it,' she cried to the others, Tracey on her knees, hands wrapped round her head, praying furiously. Jeff's fists were up ready to take on the shadows and Vince was contorting his face into the ugliest of masks to scare them off . . .

'Mirrors, he can't stand mirrors! Jeff! The one on the wall!'

'Don't touch that or . . .' shouted Mr Magus.

'Or you'll what? Something *really* horrible, you wicked old man?'

Charlie felt strong. They had weapons, too. The four of them, the Nutters, could fight back.

But he reared up, tall and threatening, drawing power from them once more.

'What I *am*,' he cried, 'you'll wish you never knew.'

He moved his hands above them, once more draining their life force. Terror almost submerged them.

'I gave you your chance. NOW give in before it's too late. GIVE IN TO ME!'

But Tracey was stirring. She loved life, her Mum, friends, clothes, school, everything. She was not going down without a struggle.

'The mirror in my bag!'

'Quick,' cried Vince.

She struggled with the zip, hands slippery with

sweat, and rummaged for the mirror, encountering make-up, tissues, notebook, keys, bracelets, packets of mints, anything but the mirror, every second a century. Then, at last, she found the mirror, hauled it out, turned it on the old man and his cat.

Gib howled.

Mr Magus stepped back.

Chapter Twenty-five

'My magnifying glass,' cried Vince, reaching for his pockets. But Mr Magus moved his hands and Vince was flattened to the floor, powerless.

Jeff had found his sunglasses and was stretching up to turn the mirror on the wall. But Mr Magus reached towards him and Jeff was halted, unable to move.

So Charlie threw herself towards the mirror, holding her specs as a shield, keeping them between her and the enemy, while Tracey with her mirror moved in behind.

Yet their power was still feeble compared with that of Mr Magus and as they faltered the shadows round the room grew stronger. A laugh sounded from somewhere, followed by its mocking echo. But the heat was now off Vince and as Charlie called:

'The magnifying glass, Vince – now,' he reached for it and turned it on Mr Magus and Gib the Cat, just as Jeff, too, summoning all his strength, and helped by Tracey and Charlie, acting together, managed to reverse the mirror on the wall.

So that Mr Magus and Gib the cat were confronted by the combined force of that mirror, Charlie's granny specs, Vince's magnifying glass, Jeff's sunglasses and Tracey's Big Bag looking glass, just as Gib the cat sprang for Charlie.

He fell back in mid-leap, back on to the floor, small, an ordinary cat once more.

Mr Magus shrank into his armchair.

'What are you doing to me?' he cried. 'I wanted to

make you good and happy.'

He gazed at them almost piteously.

Gib had grown thin, meagre.

'Why are you killing us?'

The old man stretched out his arms.

'I wanted to look after you.'

Tracey, soft-hearted, was weakening.

'Mr Magus,' she began . . .

'Stay with me. For ever . . .'

'Don't weaken,' cried Charlie. 'Hold those mirrors. If you ever want to get away from here! Tracey! Jeff!!'

'Remember the Nutters,' cried Vince.

They focused the mirrors on to Mr Magus and Gib once more.

The room darkened. A rumble of thunder could be heard, and the sound of the wind rising, gusting the trees.

With it came the noise of traffic. The outside world was coming nearer.

A piercing scream came from the old man. Or was it the cat? It held a note of infinite sadness and pain.

A flash of lightning in the room extinguished the last of the shadows as the whole room was lit up in a white surreal glow in which Mr Magus was illuminated, and then, more rapidly than the eye could take in, crumbled away to nothing.

As they watched in disbelief Gib the cat shot through the door and disappeared.

Chapter Twenty-six

Down the stairs pelted the children as if chased by demons, which indeed they thought they were. And for once in his life Vince was leading the way.

Charlie, coming last, looked back . . . at the room at the top of the house . . . the eyrie, where Mr Magus had waited for them.

Through the house they ran, bent on escape, past the bathroom, the conservatory and into the garden room where the door with its broken glass stood open.

They rushed into the garden, Jeff pausing only to grab the football lying on the carpet as he too ran outside.

As they fled, Charlie tripped and fell, and was seized with a terror worse than any she'd known so far.

'Don't leave me here! Wait for me!' she cried.

But Jeff turned back and pulled her to her feet.

'We won't leave you, Charlie girl,' he said. 'We stick together, don't we? Always.'

Ahead of them Vince was pounding away, breaking all records, heading for the fence at the bottom of the garden.

Chapter Twenty-seven

Safe at last on top of the fence, out of breath, exhausted, but with Millington Park safely in front of them, they looked back for the last time to see . . .

an old ruined house, an overgrown garden and in the distance a skinny black cat picking its way through the jungly undergrowth.